VICTRICIA MALICIA

BOOK-LOVING BUCCANEER

Written by Carrie Clickard   Illustrated by Mark Meyers

Flash
Light PRESS

For Kasidy — the best first mate that
I could have asked for. —MM

To Mom and Dad — who set my ship sailing,
Becky, Barb, and Brent — the steadfast companions
on my voyage, and Lisa W. — who gave me
the courage to brave the open seas. —CC

Copyright © 2012
by Flashlight Press
Text copyright © 2012
by Carrie Clickard
Illustrations copyright © 2012
by Mark Meyers

Library of Congress Control
Number: 2011937321

ISBN 978-1-9362611-2-3

Editor: Shari Dash Greenspan
Graphic Design: The Virtual Paintbrush

This book was typeset in Caslon Antique. The illustrations were
rendered in acrylic and mixed media on watercolor paper.

Distributed by IPG

Flashlight Press • 527 Empire Blvd. • Brooklyn, NY 11225
www.FlashlightPress.com   www.VictriciaMalicia.com

Victricia Malicia Calamity Barrett
was born on the deck of the *Potbellied Parrot*.
Her mom was the captain. Her dad, the ship's cook.
Her grandma was proud of her peg leg and hook.
But despite a tradition since sixteen-o-three
for every last Barrett to set out to sea,
plund'ring and looting
and pirate pursuiting,
Victricia detested it vehemently.
Victricia Malicia was sick of the sea.

You can't blame her fam'ly. They raised her up right.
They gave her a name filled with menace and fright.

Her cradle was shipshape.
Her blankie was black.

She learned her first words
from a parrot named Jack.

She
took
her
first
steps
off
the
rickety
plank...

...and learned to tie knots
with her old Uncle Hank.

She counted doubloons
on nights with full moons,

and spent many months with
Ye Olde Pirate Creed,
patiently teaching herself
how to read.

But though she'd grown up among seagulls and gills,
Vic never perfected her pirating skills.
She fell from the rigging, tied knots that would slip.

Her cooking caused rats to abandon the ship.

When choosing tattoos, the designs she adored
were never a skull or a blood-dripping sword.
The stickers she'd pick
made her shipmates feel sick!

And her books about life without mainsails and rudders
gave all of her pirate relations the shudders.

"I gag when my lunch is Spaghetti Tentacular —
hate when my sisters speak pirate vernacular —
want a new pet that's not scaly or spiny —
and wish I could keep my books somewhere less briny!"

She made her whole family gasp in alarm
when, for her next birthday, Vic asked for a farm.
    Her shirt — sewn by hand —
    shouted "I LOVE DRY LAND."
Her landlubber thinking was quite problematic.
Aye, V.M.C. Barrett was most un-piratic.

One morning, the pirates returned from their robbing
and found Vic on deck with a mop and pail, swabbing
with soap she created from squid spit and lotion,
which slid half the crew from the deck to the ocean,
along with three cannons,
six trunks with brass hitches...

...and seventeen pairs of the
captain's silk britches!
    Her horrible blunder
    had sunk all their plunder!
This latest mistake left the
pirates no doubt —
their patience with Vic had
completely run out.

Vic worried and paced as the ship rocked and leaned
while, deep in the hold, Pirate Council convened.
In sad but unanimous voices they voted:
"Victricia Malicia must now be de-boated!"
"Let's ground her awhile –" "For a week –" "Maybe two –"
"On a boring old island, with nothing to do."
     "Twill heighten her gratitude."
        "Fix her pirattitude!"
"Cure her strange longing for books and dry land!"
"Aye, she'll beg to come back to our buccaneer band."

So leaving her parrot,
her patch, and her pegs
(which hadn't been used,
since she still had two legs),
Vic lowered a rowboat
to head for the shore
when a sea monster burst
through the waves with a roar!
"'Tis Scylla the Serpent,
the Scourge of the Sea!
That black-hearted beast
wants a pirate for tea!"

With a flick of her tail
Scylla sliced the main sail,
then rose from the foam like a dark scaly tower,
and burst t'ward the ship with gargantuan power.

She lunged for the mast, but her slithery neck
slip-slapped on the soap Vic had sloshed on the deck,
straight into the ropes Vic had tied much too loose,
which knotted around Scylla's neck like a noose.

The Sea Serpent let out
a bloodcurdling howl
and got her head wrapped in
a skull and bones towel.

Vic hoisted her trunk,
gave the beast's head a thunk,
then sent Scylla back where the deep water churned.
The serpent slid off and she never returned!

"HuzZAH!" cried the pirates, from smallest to tall.
"Victricia Malicia has rescued us all!"
"We can't send our savior away in a boat
when she is the hero who kept us afloat!"
"Instead of marooning her, let's throw a party,
play Bottle the Ship, Pin the Sword on Me Hearty!"
        With much lighter hearts
        they unfurled their great charts,
                and plotted a course
                for the tropical village
                where Great-Grandma Barrett
                first buried their pillage.

PIN the SWORD
on
Me He

One moment of glory was all that Vic needed.
She turned to her buccaneer fam'ly and pleaded:

"I've never fit into the pirating mold.
I hate being ruthless, despise being bold.
I just want a home where the ground doesn't billow,
no fish in my bathtub or slugs on my pillow.
    I'd truly adore
      to be left here on shore.
Come back in a month with the whole Barrett clan
to see my magnificent landlubbing plan."

Ye Olde
Towne →

That tropical town was the place of her dreams.
No portholes. No hammocks. No sword fights or screams.
Vic opened a bookstore for young lads and lasses
with Sea Story Hours and A-B-C classes.

And when they're in port, every Barrett relation
makes Landlubber Books their preferred destination.
They're learning to read
at a rollicking speed,
and though they're still pirates
they're not quite barbarians —

NOW they're the world's first
seafaring librarians!